354440
j STI
Stilto
Mighty

D0251713

SAVONA LIBRARY

Dear mouse friends,
Welcome to the world of

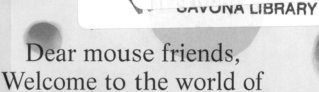

Geronimo Stilton

THE RODENT'S GAZETTE
EDITORIAL STAFF

Geronimo Stilton
A learned and brainy
mouse; editor of
The Rodent's Gazette

Thea Stilton
Geronimo's sister and
special correspondent at
The Rodent's Gazette

Trap Stilton
An awful joker;
Geronimo's cousin and
owner of the store
Cheap Junk for Less

Benjamin Stilton
A sweet and loving
nine-year-old mouse;
Geronimo's favorite
nephew

Geronimo Stilton

MIGHTY MOUNT KILIMANJARO

Scholastic Inc.

New York   Toronto   London   Auckland

Sydney   Mexico City   New Delhi   Hong Kong

Thompson-Nicola Regional District
Library System
300 · 465 VICTORIA STREET
KAMLOOPS, B.C.   V2C 2A9

If you purchased this book without a cover, you should be aware that this book is stolen property. It was reported as "unsold and destroyed" to the publisher, and neither the author nor the publisher has received any payment for this "stripped book."

No part of this book may be reproduced, stored in a retrieval system, or transmitted in any form or by any means, electronic, mechanical, photocopying, recording, or otherwise, without written permission of the copyright holder. For information regarding permission, please contact Atlantyca S.p.A., Via Leopardi 8, 20123 Milan, Italy, e-mail: foreignrights@atlantyca.it, www.atlantyca.com

3 5444 00022315 5

CHEDDAR CHEWS OR MOZZARELLA MUFFINS?

It was a chilly October evening. A tail-rattling *wind was roaring* through the streets of New Mouse City. I shivered and buttoned my jacket up to my snout. Then I locked the door to my office and started home at a brisk scamper.

Oh, excuse me, I almost forgot to introduce myself. My name is Stilton, *Geronimo Stilton*. I run *The Rodent's Gazette*, the most *famouse* newspaper on Mouse Island.

I couldn't wait to be home at 8 Mouseford Lane. FROSTY cheese pops, it was cold outside!

As soon as I opened the door, I sighed with relief. It was so cozy and warm inside my mouse hole!

I hurried into the bathroom and ran a hot bath. Ahh, there's nothing *better* than a good soak on a cold autumn evening!

After my bath, I put on my favorite flannel pajamas and slippers. Rubbing my paws in satisfaction, I opened the fridge.

Yum, yum, yum! There was so much to choose from! Should I have cheddar chews or mozzarella muffins?

Monterey Jack pie or Swiss fondue? Three-cheese pizza or baked Parmesan cheesecake? **They were all so delicious**, it was difficult to pick just one!

Since I was unable to make up my mind, I decided to treat myself. I grabbed the *largest* plate I could find and filled it with a selection of every **tasty** tidbit inside the fridge. Then I made a cup of hot cheddar and headed to the living room to light the fire.

A huge jigsaw **puzzle** was sprawled on the dining table. It was a map of New Mouse

City, and it was **tRicky** with a capital **T**!

I had been working on the **puzzle** for months, and I was just a few pieces away from completing it. I was savoring these last moments.

I might frame it and hang it up, I thought. *It's not every day a mouse gets to finish a jigsaw as challenging as this one!*

I set down my cup of cheese and looked at the remaining pieces. In went one, then another, then another. Whiskers tingling, I inserted the very **L A S T** piece.

MY JIGSAW PUZZLE!

At that very moment, the table started to tremble. I looked around in panic. Was it an earthquake? No, the rest of the room was motionless. I tried to keep the table still, but it was no good. It gave a sudden Jerk, and the puzzle exploded into a thousand pieces.

"NOOOOOOOOO!" I cried, tearing at my fur. Months of work destroyed in seconds!

Then I heard a cry: "Geronimooooooo!" My snout turned whiter than a slice of mozzarella. I had bigger problems than my ruined puzzle.

I recognized that squeak instantly. It belonged to the world's most adventurous mouse: BRUCE HYENA!

YOU'RE TOTALLY OUT OF SHAPE!

Before I could find a place to hide, my **megamuscular, megafit, megatrained, mega-energetic** friend Bruce leaped on top of the table. He grinned at me.

I groaned inwardly. Bruce is a dear friend of mine and a very caring rodent. But he lives for adventure and he loves dragging me along with him. I just don't have the tailbone for the kinds of excitement Bruce lives for.

"So, **Champ**, are you ready for our next challenge?" Bruce asked.

I shook my snout. "Oh, no. Not this time. First of all, I am **NEVER** ready for one of your crazy challenges, Bruce. And secondly,

you've just **RUINED** my favorite kind of challenge — the jigsaw I've been working on for the last six months!"

Bruce pretended not to hear me. He circled me with a critical look on his snout.

"Hmm, saggy tail . . . **DROOPY** muscles . . . cheese gut . . . you're totally out of shape!"

I tried to hide my plate of goodies behind my back. "Well, yes, but . . ."

Bruce reached around and pulled the plate out of my paws. "Ah-hah! Now I know how you stay in shape, **Cheese Puff**! You exercise your paws by opening the fridge door! You train your jawbone with your constant chewing! You keep in shape by licking your whiskers!"

He paused to sniff at the cheese. "Well, where we're going, you can forget all about these tasty morsels!"

I gulped nervously. "Wh- where do you want to take me, Bruce?"

Bruce folded his paws across his brawny chest. "A little place with rocks, snow, and ice. A little place that's 19,340 feet above sea level. A little place called MOUNT KILIMANJARO, where Cheesy Chews are nothing but a distant memory!"

"MOUNT KILIMANJARO?" I cried. "Oh, no. Absolutely not. Bruce, if you think I'm coming to Mount Kilithingummy, the CHEESE must have slipped off your CRACKER!" I exclaimed. "You have *Geronimo Stilton's* word on that!"

I'M A BOOKMOUSE,
NOT A
SPORTSMOUSE!

"This was your sister Thea's *idea*," Bruce said. "She said it would make a G R E A T scoop!"

Without another squeak, I rushed to the phone and called my sister.

"Thea, I beg you, pleeeeeeease don't send me to **MOUNT KILIMANJARO**! I'm a **bookmouse**, not a sportsmouse!"

"Now, Geronimo, I don't want to hear any whining," she replied briskly. "You know that sales of the paper double when we publish one of your travelogues!"

She was right. My sister was right about almost everything. It was one of her most **IRRITATING** qualities. "Yes, but —"

"No buts now," Thea interrupted. "Do you want to **disappoint** your readers?"

She had me there. There was nothing I hated more than disappointing my readers. "No, but —"

Then Thea pawed the phone over to my dear nephew Benjamin. "Uncle Geronimo! I heard you're going to climb **MOUNT KILIMANJARO**! You're so **brave**! When I'm older, I want to be just like you! Will you send me a postcard?"

I gave up. The only thing I hated more than disappointing my readers was disappointing my nephew. "Yes, Benjamin. I'll climb **MOUNT KILIMANJARO** and I'll bring you back a souvenir!"

Now, Where's my Thank-You?

A few minutes later, **BRUCE** dragged me out of my mouse hole. We were off to the best sports store in New Mouse City, Rats Authority.

Bruce strode into the store and blew an obnoxiously loud whistle: Phweeeeeeeeeeeeeeeeeeeee!

I cowered behind him as he started shouting. "Come on! Look sharp, all of you! Hup-hup-hup! Move those paws! This is an **EMEEEEEEEEEEEEEEEERGENCY!**"

The manager (who knows me well) and his sales clerks all scurried to the counter.

"What's happening? An emergency? Where?" they shouted.

Bruce pulled out a list as long as a muskrat's tail. "**Come on then**, smarty-fur! We've got a date with Mount Kilimanjaro. We need ONE tent! TWO sleeping bags! THreE bottles of sunblock! FOUr pairs of gloves! FiVe packets of blister cushions . . . actually, better make that SiX, because there are miles, miles, and Miiiiiiiiiiiiles to be covered!"

The manager looked at us as if we were out of our minds! My fur went **RED** with embarrassment. I tried to hide behind Bruce. He's so **BRAWNY**, he provides good cover.

The manager and his sales clerks all scurried around. A few minutes later, we were ready to check out.

The sales clerk printed out a receipt that was longer than Bruce's list. When I saw the number at the bottom, I turned as pale as goat cheese.

sleeping bag

hiking boots

sweater

clogs

guide to Kenya & Tanzania

camera

waterproof pants

coat

fleece shirt

flashlight

long underwear

wool socks

headlamp

shirts and T-shirts

canteen

bandanna

ski mask

survival kit

gloves

sweatsuit

travel diary and pen

towels

underwear

sunglasses

mirror

sunblock

hat

first aid kit

toothbrush, comb, toothpaste, and soap

passport and vaccination certificate

backpack

Swahili mini-dictionary

Bruce winked at the sales clerk. "Put it all on **Cheesehead**'s tab — I mean, Mr. Stilton's account. He's **LOADED**! Bye for now — we'll see you before our next adventure!"

With that, he marched out of the store, calling back to me, "That's the way to do it! **Take a leaf out of my book, champ**! Now, where's my thank-you?"

I opened my snout, though not to say thank you. Before I could get a squeak in edgewise, Bruce was yammering away again.

"Now, **Cheese Puff**, there's one last thing: Is your will up-to-date? Have you chosen a nice coffin? Have you booked a place at the local graveyard? Just in case we never come back. Adventurous journeys like this one can sometimes go **wrong**, you know."

My whiskers trembled with horror. At that moment, my cell phone *rang*.

LEAVE YOUR BURIAL TO ME, GERONIMO!

It was **BORIS VON CACKLEFUR**, my friend **CREEPELLA'S** father and owner of Fabumouse Funerals. "I understand you're going to climb **MOUNT KILIMANJARO**, Geronimo," he squealed. "Don't worry about anything. If you happen to die, leave your burial arrangements to me. I'll make sure you get a classy funeral. I've got a gorgeous yellow coffin I've been saving especially for you!"

I could feel the blood draining out of my tail. "Oh, well, that's very nice of you, but I'm sure it won't be necessary."

Ouch!

Boris **SNICKERED**. "Hee hee hee, who can tell? **MOUNT KILIMANJARO** is 19,340 feet high — I checked Gouda Maps — and all sorts of things can happen on the way up. You might break your paw, fall into a crevice, freeze to death . . ."

Heeeeelp!

CREEPELLA snatched the phone away from her father. Do you know Creepella von Cacklefur? She's a charming rodent with just two

Brrrr!

defects. This first is that she insists she is my fiancée, which is completely untrue. And the second is that she is far too **SPOOKY** for me! I'm way too big a 'fraidy mouse to marry a creepy rodent like Creepella.

"Now listen up, my sweet little bat wing," Creepella squeaked. "You've got to come back alive, all right? I've got big plans for our future, you know! There'll be trouble in store for you if you kick the bucket on **MOUNT**

Do you know Creepella von Cacklefur? She insists she is my fiancée, which is completely untrue...

KILIMANJARO. After the engagement, we're getting married! Got it?"

Bruce punched me playfully on the arm. I flinched. "Why, aren't you the sneaky little **cheese puff**! You didn't tell me you were engaged!"

"I'm not engaged," I tried to explain.

"And you certainly didn't tell me you were thinking about getting *married*!" Bruce continued.

"But I'm **NOT** thinking about getting married!" I protested.

"Good morning, Creepella," he yelled into the phone. "Don't worry, I'll make sure your future husband is back for the engagement — sorry, marriage — celebration! He'll be a real he-mouse by the time we return, just you wait and see!"

Bruce snapped the phone shut. Then he

dug an elbow into my ribs, leaving behind a bruise the size of a cheese Danish. "So when's the honeymoon, **Cheesehead**?"

"**NEVER.** Rodent's honor."

Bruce sighed. "I know all about being in love . . . I'm head over paws in love with your sister." A WISTFUL look came over his snout. Suddenly, he brightened up. "Hey, here's an **ideaaaaa**! Let's make it a double wedding! You and Creepella, me and Thea!"

My phone beeped. It was a text from Creepella: "**GHOSTIE-WHOSTIE, YOU'LL BE IN BIG TROUBLE IF YOU DON'T COME BACK SAFE AND SOUND. LOVE AND NIBBLES, CREEPELLA.**"

In despair, I wondered what was more dangerous: climbing to the top of **MOUNT KILIMANJARO** or facing Creepella when I returned!!!

A ONCE-IN-A-LIFETIME ADVENTURE!

The next morning, we boarded a plane to Tanzania. When the flight attendant came along with my lunch, **BRUCE** snatched the tray from under my snout.

"Listen up, **Champ**, you're on a diet as of today. A d-i-e-t, understood? You'll never get to the top of **KILIMANJARO** unless you start losing that cheese gut!"

Bruce turned to the other passengers. "Hey, everyone! **Cheese Puff** here is going to climb Mount Kilimanjaro. That's nothing to sneeze at, rodents!"

Everyone was staring at us. I *BLUSHED* from the tip of my snout to the tip of my

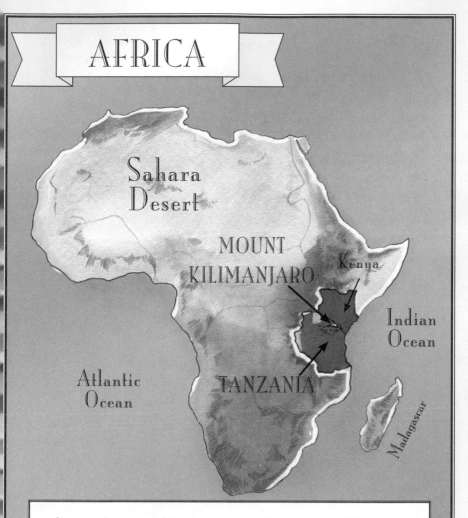

AFRICA

Sahara
Desert

MOUNT
KILIMANJARO

Kenya

Indian
Ocean

Atlantic
Ocean

TANZANIA

Madagascar

Africa is the second largest continent in the world. Its total surface area is more than 11.6 million square miles. It contains the world's longest river — the Nile River, the world's largest desert — the Sahara Desert, and the world's highest free-standing mountain — Mount Kilimanjaro.

Mount Kilimanjaro is actually a dormant volcano. It rises to a height of 19,340 feet. It is located in Tanzania, near the equator. It is the tallest walkable mountain in the world!

To climb Kilimanjaro, you leave the savannah and then walk through a dense rain forest. After that, you reach the moors, followed by an immense expanse of volcanic rock. Finally, you get to the often snowcapped peak with breathtaking views of clouds, cliffs, and plains.

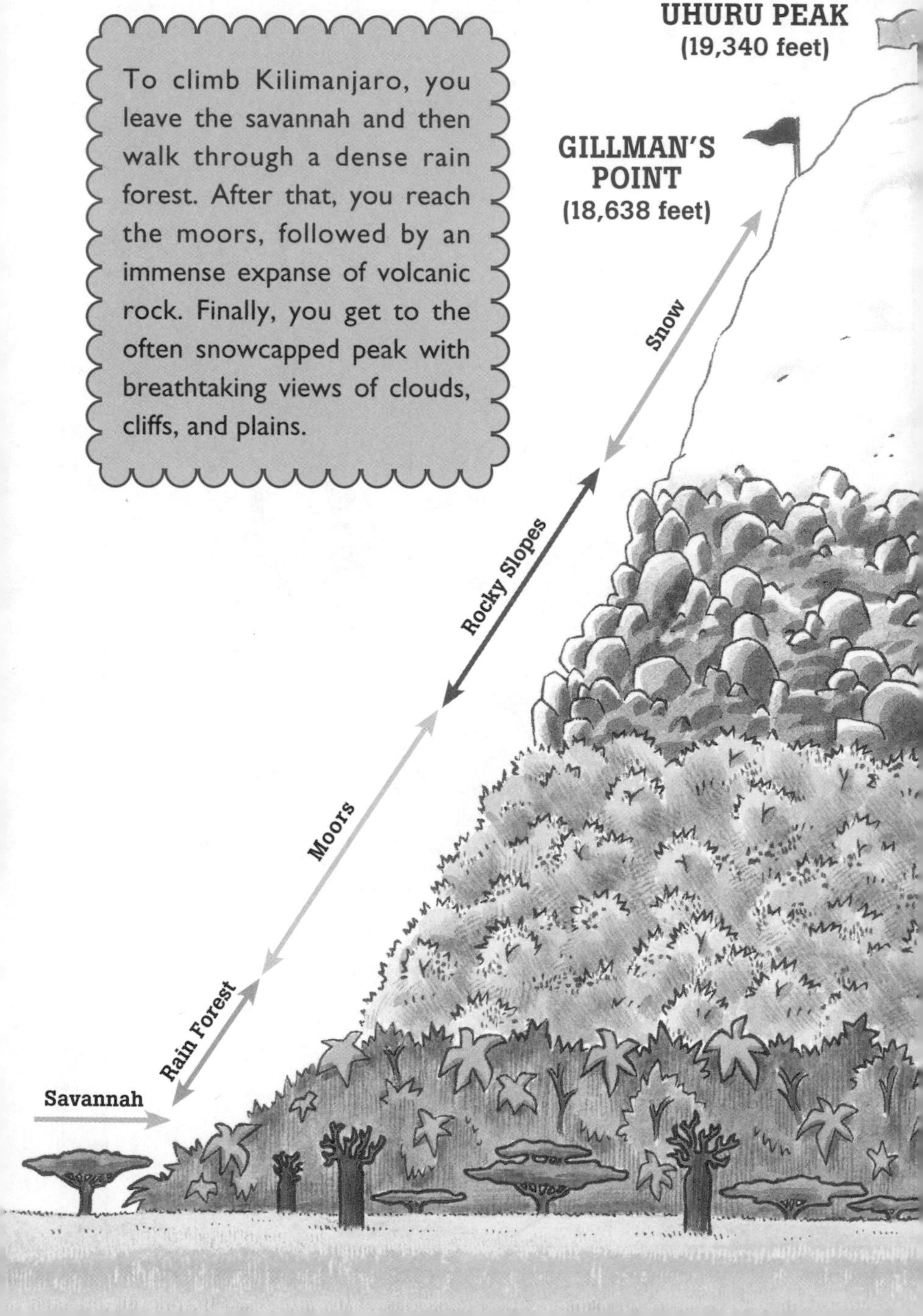

UHURU PEAK
(19,340 feet)

GILLMAN'S POINT
(18,638 feet)

Snow

Rocky Slopes

Moors

Rain Forest

Savannah

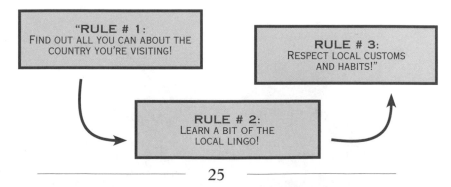

tail. But I was used to it. When you hang out with **BRUCE**, you're always at the center of attention.

"Okay, Cheesehead, it's time for my **TRAVEL TIPS**," he rattled on.

I gave him a funny look. Did Bruce think I'd just fallen off the **cheese cart**? Sure, I hated traveling, but I'd been doing it for years!

Bruce shook his snout sadly. "I don't know, if I wasn't here to educate you . . . well, where's my thank-you? Come on, I'll teach you a few words of Swahili. Repeat after me . . ."

"**RULE # 1:**
FIND OUT ALL YOU CAN ABOUT THE COUNTRY YOU'RE VISITING!

RULE # 2:
LEARN A BIT OF THE LOCAL LINGO!

RULE # 3:
RESPECT LOCAL CUSTOMS AND HABITS!"

MINI-DICTIONARY

Hello: *Hujambo*
Welcome: *Karibu*
Good-bye: *Kwa heri*
How are you?: *Habari gani?*
Fine, thanks: *Mzuri*
Good night: *Lala salama*
Yes: *Ndiyo*
No: *Hapana*
Thank you: *Asante*
Thanks very much: *Asante sana*
No problem: *Hakuna matata*
Slow and steady: *Polepole*
What's your name?: *Unaitwa nani?*

OF SWAHILI

Today: *Leo*
Tomorrow: *Kesho*
Toilet: *Choo*
Food: *Chakula*
Water: *Maji*
Vegetables: *Mboga*
Banana: *Ndizi*
Meat: *Nyama*
Milk: *Maziwa*
Bread: *Mkate*
Chicken: *Kuku*
Rice: *Mchele*
Egg: *Yai*

Swahili is the official language of Tanzania. It is also spoken in Kenya, Zanzibar, Uganda, the Democratic Republic of Congo, Zambia, Mozambique, Malawi, Rwanda and Burundi, Somalia, and the Comoro Islands.

Numbers

1	moja	6	sita
2	mbili	7	saba
3	tatu	8	nane
4	nne	9	tisa
5	tano	10	kumi

THE DEADLY RAIN FOREST!

At last, we landed at **KILIMANJARO** International Airport in **Tanzania**. Our guide, **Baraka**, a DIGNIFIED-LOOKING rodent, was there to meet us: *"Karibu (welcome)!"*

I was so pleased to be able to say something back in Swahili: *"Hujambo, habari gani (hello, how are you)?"*

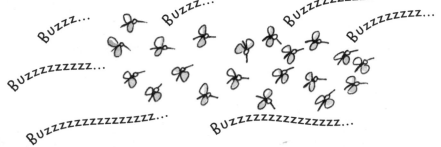

We got on a minibus and bumped and rattled along for a few hours before arriving in Marangu, at the foot of **MOUNT KILIMANJARO**. We were already six thousand feet above sea level!

I gazed at the mountain. It looked like an **enormouse rounded** cone. It reminded me of a doughnut sprinkled with iced cheese.

Mmmmm . . . the thought of cheese made my tummy rumble! But I knew if I squeaked up all I'd get was another lecture about my **cheddar** belly.

So I adjusted my backpack and Bruce, Baraka, and I headed for the forest, where we were greeted by an unbelievable buzzing sound.

Buzzz... Buzz... Buzz... Buzzzzzzzzzzzzz... Buzzzzzzzz... Buzzzzzzzzz... Buzzzzzzzzzzzzzzz... Buzzzzzzzzzzzzzzz...

YOU CALL THOSE MOSQUITOES?

What could be making that sound? It was as loud as a chain saw.

"*Hakuna matata* (no problem)," **Baraka** reassured me. "**They're only mosquitoes!**"

The mosquitoes swarmed around us. The insect cloud was so **thick**, I could hardly see Bruce and Baraka. The mosquitoes were so huge, they looked like helicopters!

"You call those mosquitoes? Ahhhhhhhhhhhh! They're biting me all over!"

I started swatting myself on the snout.

But that just made it worse:
My snout started swelling
up like a big red balloon!
The itching was unbearable.

As we climbed the mountain,
the vegetation changed, thankfully! Soon
we had left the mosquitoes behind.

I tried not to think about my swollen snout
as I trudged along the muddy path. It was so
hot! My paws were aching, and I was short
of breath.

BRUCE glanced back at me. "Come on,
Champ, move those paws! The first day is
always the hardest. Once you've warmed up
those puny little muscles of yours, you'll be fine."

Baraka pointed toward the forest.
"This forest is home to Cape buffaloes,
rhinoceroses, leopards, and monkeys," he
told us.

Rain Forest

1 RHINOCEROS
2 CROCODILE
3 LEOPARD
4 HIPPOPOTAMUS
5 MARABOU STORK
6 OKAPI
7 GUENON
8 TREE PANGOLIN

9 PYTHON
10 MANDRILL
11 CAPE BUFFALO
12 DUIKER
13 RED RIVER HOG
14 MOUNTAIN
   GORILLA

"And snakes, too!" added **BRUCE**. "So keep your eyes peeled, **Cheese Puff**!"

S-s-snakes? I gulped nervously. That was way worse than mosquitoes!

As we scampered along, *SUNLIGHT* filtered through the branches of the huge trees above.

Curdled cream cheese, my paws were really aching! I wondered how many blisters I had. I sat down to take off my boots.

I was so absorbed in my paws, I didn't even notice something **cool** and **SLiMY** was slithering over me — until it wrapped itself around my neck!! It squeezed so tight, I turned purple. By the time **BRUCE** popped out

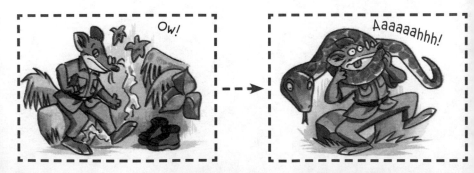

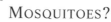

from behind a bush, my eyes were bulging.

"Well, well, well, **Champ**, look at the mess you've gotten yourself into now! This snake is made of RUBBER, but if it had been real . . . well, let's just say you're *lucky* to have me around to teach you. Where's my thank-you?"

What?! I couldn't believe it! I was ANGRIER than a fat house cat who's missed feeding time! Bruce just laughed. "Why, I didn't know you could run so fast, Cheesehead! Run run run!"

I chased Bruce here, there, and everywhere until we reached the Mandara Huts at nine thousand feet!

A Magical Vegetable Soup

After our four-hour trek, it was finally time for dinner. I was so hungry, I could've eaten MOLDY cheese rinds.

Baraka took us to a wooden hut full of fellow climbers. There we discovered that MOUNT KILIMANJARO (or **Kili**, as it is affectionately known) is a very popular destination with mountaineers. There were rodents from all over the world, and the hut echoed with squeaking in many different languages.

As I chatted with my fellow climbers, I quickly learned that despite our different backgrounds, we all had something in common: our *love* of the mountains and our desire to overcome our personal limitations.

Baraka prepared a **delicious** vegetable soup. *"Chakula* (food)!" he announced.

This soup smells great, but I could really go for a **three-cheese pizza** *right now,* I thought. Bruce slurped the soup down in one big gulp, then rubbed his belly and said, "YUMMMMMMM!"

I smiled at Baraka. *"Asante* (thank you)!" The hot soup restored my strength. Now I was ready for a nice, long ratnap. I climbed into my sleeping bag and was sound asleep before I could begin counting hamsters.

THE MOORS!

The next morning, **Baraka** woke us at dawn. After a cup of hot cheddar and a bowl of oatmeal, we set off again.

The rain forest gradually gave way to moors covered in heather and giant groundsels. It was beautiful.

Baraka **POINTED** out a tiny chameleon.

It changed color so quickly!

I stared at it in wonder. I wished Benjamin was there to see it. He would've been amazed.

Heather

Groundsel

Chameleon

POLEPOLE . . . SLOW AND STEADY!

The moors soon gave way to grass six feet high that swayed in the wind. The way it moved reminded me of WAVES on the ocean.

"As we climb upward, the amount of oxygen in the air diminishes," **Baraka** explained. "You'll notice that we'll get tired quickly. If you want to make it to the top of Mount Kilimanjaro, there's only one way to do it: slow and steady."

He repeated the idea in Swahili: "*Polepole*

(slow and steady)! We're in no hurry. We'll go slow and steady — very slow and steady! *Polepole . . . polepole . . . polepole . . .*"

Bruce and I nodded in agreement. I could tell **Baraka** knew what he was doing, and I was glad Bruce had found such a good guide.

As we continued our trek, we were soon overtaken by other groups going **FASTER** than us. They looked down their snouts at us, but Baraka just winked and said: "*Polepole, hakuna matata* (slow and steady, no problem)!"

ARE WE THERE YET?

We went on that way for hours and hours. **"Are we there yet?"** I moaned in exhaustion. "It feels like we've been hiking forever!"

"You'll know we're there when you see the lobelias," explained **Baraka**. "Lobelias are succulent plants with fleshy, pointed leaves. They grow at ten thousand feet."

I looked carefully at every plant we encountered, but I couldn't find a lobelia to save my fur!

"Lobelia?" I asked hopefully as we passed plants here and there. But Baraka just shook his snout.

Hours passed. They felt like **D A Y S**. Baraka was right — I was definitely getting tired quickly.

Finally, **BRUCE** pointed to a plant half-hidden by the grass. "Lobeliaaaaaaa!" I looked around and saw several other similar plants. They were all huge, some even taller than I was. Those bizarre-looking plants reminded me of a prehistoric forest. I half expected a dinosaur to come stomping by!

It grew *misty* as the day stretched on. But soon I made out a cluster of tiny triangular huts clinging to the mountain like fleas to a cat's fur. We'd arrived at the Horombo Huts at 12,200 feet.

Lobeliaaaaaaaaaaaaaaaaaaaa!

It was only our second day, but my paws were already lined with blisters. **Crusty kitty litter, I was in agony!**

I had something to eat, and I wanted to go straight to bed, but first I had to write in my travel **DIARY**. When I got back to New Mouse City, I wanted to be able to describe everything that had happened as accurately as possible. That way, my readers would *feel* like they'd climbed **MOUNT KILIMANJARO** along with me.

A WASTELAND OF VOLCANIC ROCK

The next morning, we were up at dawn again. I felt as if I could have slept another twelve hours, but a cup of HOT cheddar and a bowl of oatmeal got my paws moving again.

A faster group overtook us. "**See you later, Slowpokes!**" They laughed. We ignored them and continued at our slow and steady pace.

After a while, the landscape became a desolate wasteland of volcanic rock. A pitiless gust of **icy** wind whipped through the boulders. Nothing grew among these bare rocks and stones. There were no plants, no flowers — nothing. The landscape was so **barren**, it was almost as if we had landed on the **MOON**!

The farther we went, the thinner the air became. It was getting more and more difficult to walk.

After a little while, we met up with the **smarty-mice** who had overtaken us earlier. They had come to a halt. Their tongues were hanging out, and they looked like they were about to **pass out**.

We passed them slowly but surely. **Baraka** shook his snout and murmured, "Mountains are not to be messed with."

Bruce nodded. "Come on, **Cheese Puff**, let's show them how real he-mice get to the top: slow and steady, tired but inspired."

KILI WILL PUT FUR ON YOUR CHEST!

I felt **dreadful**. My snout was sunburned because I hadn't used enough sunblock at this high altitude. But what was really getting to me was that my tummy was all topsy-turvy!

As for **BRUCE**, he chatted away like there was no tomorrow. Didn't his jawbone ever get tired? I wondered if he exercised that, too!

"Just wait and see, **Champ**, climbing **KILI** will put fur on your chest! After this, you'll be ready to climb anything." I was too exhausted to speak. All I could manage was a long groan: "**AAAAAAAAAAAGHHHHH!**"

Bruce laughed. "Come on, Cheesehead! Keep your eyes on the prize. Let's concentrate on making it to the top. **COME ON, COME ON, COME ON!**"

Then he launched into a song he'd made up: "The Kilimanjaro Song."

We'll get to the top of Kilimanjaro,
It's not really all that far-oh!
Who knows if we'll come through alive,
But hey, why shouldn't we survive?
Our actions louder than words that squeak
We aren't afraid of an ol' mountain peak!
We're mice, we're tough, and we're not gonna stop!
Till we get to that snowcapped mountaintop!

"Aaaaaaaaaagh!" I whimpered. "But I *am* afraid. And I *do* want to survive!"

BRUCE was taken aback. "But you've

already made your will, haven't you? You've chosen your **COFFIN**, and your place in the graveyard has been booked, right? So what are you worried about? Think about the glory of snuffing it on **Kili**'s barren slopes! Think about how famouse you'll be. Imagine the headline: **Read all about it! Geronimo Stilton, editor of *THE RODENT'S GAZETTE*, lost on Kilimanjaro!** Don't you want to be famouse, Geronimo?"

"Bruce, I'd rather be famouse for my life than my death!" I replied.

MAKE IT MENTAL!

"You're exhausted, aren't you?" asked Bruce. "You've got a **cramp** in your paws, right? Well, when it feels like you can't go on, make it **MENTAL**!"

I had no idea what he was squeaking about now. "What do you mean?" I asked.

He flicked me on the snout. "It's all inside your head! Everything starts upstairs, you know. Feeling tired is a mental problem, you have **BRUCE HYENA'S WORD** on that! Come on, repeat after me: forward, forward, forward, forward ... forward, forward, forward ... forward, forward ..."

I gave him the **DIRTIEST** look I could muster. Didn't he ever quit? Well, I guess I already knew the answer to that one.

No, he didn't.

An Absolutely
Gorgeous Rodent

All of a sudden, I heard a *sweet* voice singing the New Mouse City anthem:

A thousand voices squeak as one,
A thousand tails proudly wag,
A thousand whiskers boldly quiver,
A thousand paws raise your yellow flag!
Under our fur, a thousand hearts beat for you,
Sweet, sweet Mouse Island.

Instinctively, I started singing along. That anthem is a work of inspiration. Just hearing it makes me straighten up my tail with pride. I turned around to see who was singing. What a **lovely** squeak!

When I laid eyes on the singer, my whiskers quivered with emotion. It was an absolutely gorgeous rodent with amber fur and eyes as bright as stars in the African sky. She shot me an *irresistible* smile.

My heart started beating faster than a rodent on the run from a hungry cat.

Boom-boom! Boom-boom! Boom-boom! Boom-boom!

I bowed and kissed her paw. She smelled of Mousey Sighs, the most delectable perfume known to rodentkind. I was so overcome by her *beauty*, I found myself stuttering: "M-mm-miss, g-g-good d-d-day to you, m-my name is S-s-s-s-s-s . . ." I was breathless, but

THOMPSON-NICOLA REGIONAL DISTRICT LIBRARY SYSTEM

whether this was because of the altitude or the **stunning creature** before me, I couldn't say!

"Hello," she said. "My name is Makeda."

"You have a splendid voice!" I said in my most high-pitched squeak.

She **smiled**. "Thank you. I'm an actress, but I adore outdoor adventures, don't you?"

Instead of agreeing with her, I chose to tell the truth: "Well, I'm more of a bookmouse

than a sportsmouse, actually. I'm here to experience this adventure so I can tell my readers at *The Rodent's Gazette* all about it when —"

Makeda squealed with delight. *"The Rodent's Gazette*? **That's my favorite newspaper!** So you must be the one and only *Geronimo Stilton*!"

If I hadn't already been SCARLET with sunburn, I would have turned a similar shade from pride and embarrassment.

"So you're climbing **Kilimanjaro** this evening, too?" Makeda asked. "Perhaps we can climb up together? If you don't mind the company, of course."

I was about to say that I would be delighted to climb with her when **BRUCE** butted in. "Good morning, miss!" he roared in his usual loud squeak. "Do excuse me if I

drag this cheesehead away."

For a moment, I thought I saw a look of disappointment cross Makeda's snout. Was it possible that she liked me? Was it possible that I was her type? Could a scrawny little bookmouse like me really win over a **GORGEOUS** supermouse like her?

I was about to protest when **BRUCE** dragged me off by the tail.

"Farewell, Makeda," I shouted. "I mean, bye-bye for now. I hope to see you soon! Best of luck! Let's get together sometime."

But it was no use. **MY CONFUSED, DESPERATE WORDS** were carried off by the freezing mountain winds.

MIDNIGHT
HORROR STORY!

We'd finally reached the Kibo Huts at 15,430 feet. My tummy was still giving me a hard time. I wanted to eat, but the altitude was really making me nauseous — the higher you climb, and the thinner the air, the more likely you are to experience nausea and dehydration.

The huts were built out of stone and corrugated iron. Inside each one, there were bunk beds for the climbers, but there was no running water. And the worst part was, it was **icy cold**!

Desperate to keep warm, I put on all the clothes I had.

When I was finished, I had on so many layers, I looked like an **overstuffed** turkey.

"Tonight is the night, my friends," said **Baraka**. "We have to leave at midnight. We must reach the summit and start coming back down again before nine o'clock in the morning. That's when the weather starts getting worse!"

I knew I should rest, but I was desperate to see Makeda again. I gave **BRUCE** a lame excuse and began scurrying around to look for her.

After an hour of fruitless searching, **BRUCE** caught

**Uhuru Peak
19,340 feet**

Two hours of hiking

**Gillman's Point
18,638 feet**

Six hours of hiking

**Kibo Huts
15,430 feet**

up with me. "Cheesehead, you're supposed to be resting! Where have you been?" he asked suspiciously.

"Don't worry, I couldn't find Makeda! I'll never see her again . . . **ever**!" I sobbed. "And it's all your fault!"

Besides being heartsick, I was still feeling sick in another part of my anatomy — my TUMMY! I knew it was a symptom of altitude sickness.

Oh, how I missed my warm, cozy mouse hole in New Mouse City!

After dinner, I tried to relax, but I just couldn't. Finally, I made my way into the big STONE room where the climbers slept. Rickety bunk beds leaned against the wall. Wearily, I climbed into my sleeping bag.

Oh, how I missed the warm comfort of my own bed!

That night was the **worst** I've ever had. The lack of oxygen made me feel like I was suffocating. It was miserable! Whenever I started to doze off, I woke up with a start. It was worse than my worst **NIGHTMARE**, the one where I'm taking the ACTs (Ancient **Cheeses** Test) and can't remember the difference between Camembert and Colby.

Ratty Chops, the mouse sleeping on the bunk below me, kept calling out in his sleep. He sounded even more miserable than I was.

At last, at the stroke of **MIDNIGHT**, our guide arrived. "Time to get up! **We've got to get going!** Move those paws!" (Bruce was starting to rub off on him, I could tell.)

Ratty Chops shook his snout in desperation. "I feel absolutely **awful**. I just can't do it.

But I'll come back next year to try again!"

"Well said, friend," said **BRUCE**. "There's true wisdom in recognizing the moment to say no. Better luck next time!"

"Well, in that case," I piped up hopefully. "I think I'll say no as well!"

"Not you, Stilton," Bruce replied. "On your paws, Cheesehead!"

Ratty Chops sighed and put a photo of a little mouse back in his backpack. "I promised my daughter that I would take her photo to the top of **MOUNT KILIMANJARO**."

BRUCE placed his paw on Ratty's shoulder. "*Hakuna matata* (no problem)! We'll do it for you. **IT'S THE LEAST WE CAN DO FOR A FRIEND!**"

DID YOU KNOW . . . ?

It was pitch-black outside. We joined a **long line** of wheezing climbers who were setting off along the uphill path.

No one squeaked. No one had the strength.

Behind me, **BRUCE** snickered: "**Cheese Puff**, if you start rolling backward, I'll catch you, okay? Tee-hee!"

I didn't laugh. I didn't have the strength.

As we worked our way slowly up the path, the amount of oxygen decreased and our **FATIGUE** increased.

While I was hauling myself along the pebbly slope, which became steeper and steeper, **BRUCE** started telling me **TERRIFYING** mountain legends.

"**DID YOU KNOW THAT** the weather can change suddenly in the mountains? **DID YOU KNOW THAT** if it changes while we're on the summit, we won't have enough time to get back down? **DID YOU KNOW THAT** someone cashes in their cheese on **Kilimanjaro** every year? But you don't need to worry about that, Champ: you've already written your will, you've chosen a **nice** casket, you've booked a place at the graveyard — you've thought of everything!"

The perfect ice cube . . .

I shivered, both from the cold and from Bruce's stories. My paws were numb. My tail was frozen stiff. I'd be the perfect **ice cube** in a yeti cocktail.

FORWARD!

Every tiny gesture drained my ENERGY. I felt like I was walking in slow motion, almost as if I were underwater! It occurred to me that I was at the same height as many airplanes — 19,000 feet!

Baraka handed me his water bottle: "*Maji* (water)? *Polepole* (slow and steady)!"

I *swallowed* half the bottle's contents in one big gulp. But the water was icy, and I realized I had made a serious mistake! Immediately, I felt sick to my stomach and **very nauseous**.

I tumbled to the ground and rolled over and over. I felt sicker than a young seamouse on his first trip on the Ratlantic.

Baraka leaned over and said kindly, "I'm

afraid that's it, Geronimo. You'll have to go back down."

BRUCE nodded. "Let's forget it for now, Geronimo. No long snouts, though — we can always try again next year!"

I was about to agree when suddenly, Benjamin's words **ECHOED** in my ears: "Uncle Geronimo, you're going to climb Mount Kilimanjaro? You're so **BRAVE**!"

I gulped . . .

the water was icy . . .

i felt sick to my stomach!

I mustered all the energy I had left. "No. Let's go forward." I muttered.

I got up slowly. **BRUCE** gave me a surprisingly ᵍᵉₙₜₗₑ paw on the back. I started walking, repeating to myself as I did so: "Forward, forward, forward, forward, forward, forward, forward . . ."

forwar
forward forwa
forward forward forw
forward forward forward fo
forward forward forward forward
forward forward forward forward forwar
forward forward forward forward forward forwa
forward forward forward forward forward forwa
forward forwardforward forward forward forward forward forwa
forward forward forward forward forward forward forward forward
ward forward forward forward forward fo ward forward forward forwar

FORWARD!

forwc
forward for
forward forward fo
forward forward forward
forward forward forward
forward forward forward forward
forward forward forward forward forwa
forward forward forward forward forward forw
forward forward forward forward forward forward fo
forward forward forward forrd forward forward forward forw
forward forward forward forward forward forward forward forward
orward forward forward forward forward forward forward forward forward
forward forward forward forward forward forward forward forward for
rd forward forward forward forward forward forward forward forward forw
rd forward forward forward forward forward forward forward forward f
ard forward forward forward forward forward forward forward forward f
orward forward forward forward forward forward forward forward forwa
d forward forward forward forward forward forward forward forward fc
d forward forward forward forward forward forward forward forward fe
ard forward forward forward forward forward forward forward forward fe
rd forward forward forward forward forward forward forward forward for
ard forward forward forward forward forward forward forward forward for
forward forward forward forward forward forward forward forward for
d forward forward forward forward forward forward forward forward for

A SPECK IN THE INFINITE UNIVERSE!

"**LOOK, GERONIMO!**" called **BRUCE**. "Look at this incredible view!"

Bruce opened his arms wide and yelled: "This is the life! I feel like a speck in the infinite universe! *Thanks for existing, world!*"

I finally looked up from the path and fell silent. **BRUCE** was right. Dawn on **Kilimanjaro** was a whisker-tingling sight. Along the horizon, the deep indigo sky was streaked with pink, violet, and orange. It was fabumouse!

BRUCE sighed. "How I wish Thea was here with me now. *You know, I'm snout over paws in love with her.*"

A whisker-tingling sight!

Thea

Benjamin

Makeda

I thought how nice it would be to have Benjamin here with me now. Perhaps he would climb **MOUNT KILIMANJARO** when he grew up.

Then my thoughts turned to **Makeda** and those *bewitching* eyes of hers. Even a 'fraidy mouse like me could find the courage for adventure with her by my side! Would I ever see her again?

Bruce hit me over the snout with a snowshoe.

"Chop-chop, Cheese Puff. Forward, forward, forward, forward, forward, forward, forward!"

THE SUMMIT
AT LAST!

I was having a really hard time with the lack of oxygen. **BRUCE** kept repeating: "Forward, forward, forward, forward, forward . . ."

His words boomed through my brain like cat claws on a hardwood floor.

Baraka pointed to the end of the path. "**Uhuru Peak!** The summit of **MOUNT KILIMANJARO**!"

We'd reached the summit!

we'd climbed **MOUNT KILIMANJARO**!

BRUCE knelt down and kissed the snow. Then he declared, "Mount Kilimanjaro, thanks for existing!"

I climbed the rest of the way to the peak very slowly. Then I shook paws with **Baraka**

and Bruce. "Thanks, my friends. I could never have made it without you!"

Baraka smiled at me. Using the timer on our camera, we took a photo of ourselves **WAVING** a Mouse Island flag and holding the photo Ratty Chops had given us.

Baraka was starting to get anxious. "All right, friends, *we've got to get back down*!"

I was ecstatically happy. Throwing my paws open wide, I gazed far into the distance and thanked my lucky stars I was alive at that moment.

Baraka shook me by the paw and said urgently, "*We have to get back down! RIGHT NOW!*" He pointed to the sky. Black clouds were looming menacingly on the horizon.

WE HAVE TO GET BACK DOWN!

Baraka's anxiety was contagious. My whiskers were quivering with fear as we hurried back down the path. I looked up at the sky. A **big, dark cloud** was getting closer and closer. That wasn't a good sign.

BRUCE's TERRIFYING stories flashed through my mind. We were about to be trapped in a storm! Our fur was at risk! Maybe I should've taken Bruce's advice and booked a place in the **graveyard**!

Instead of his usual *polepole,* Baraka was urging us to get a move on: "*We have to keep moving!*"

As he squeaked, the **sun** disappeared

behind a mass of **INKY** black clouds. Faster than you could say "frosty cheese pops with crumbs on top," the weather had changed. The icy wind that swept across the mountain was so **wicked**, it almost blew me over!

Going down was easier than going up. But Baraka pointed out that it could be too easy. We didn't want to trip and **SLIDE DOWN**. "Watch your step!" he reminded us.

I was trying to be careful, I really was. But suddenly, I slipped on a **ROCKY** crag covered in ice.

My paws flailed in the air as I desperately tried to find something to hold on to.

It was too late. I fell down, down, down.

"**Bruce, help!**" I yelled. He tried to grab me by the tail, but then he slipped, too!

"Don't **WORRY**, Champ!" he shouted. "Sooner or later, we've got to **HIT BOTTOM**!"

"That's what I'm afraid of!" I shouted back. We could tumble down 19,340 feet — from the top of **Mount Kilimanjaro** to the **BOTTOM**!

This was going to be one heck of a nosedive, I could feel it in my **fur**!

ROLLING, ROLLING, ROLLING!

As we plunged downward, **BRUCE** shouted: "We're **P** **I** **B** **T** (**P**robably **I**n **B**ig **T**rouble)!"

"It's worse than that!" I replied. "I reckon we're **DAD** (**D**ead **A**s **D**oornails)!"

We rolled, rolled, rolled, rolled, rolled, rolled down Mount Kilimanjaro!

After one last **fur-raising** leap through the air, we ended up snout-down in a mound of volcanic dust. We had stopped! **Miraculously**, we had stopped!

I was covered in snow and dust from the tip of my tail to the ends of my whiskers.

"**BRUCE**, are you alive?" I spluttered. I looked around me. Nothing. No sign of Bruce. Until . . . wait, was that his tail sticking up behind a **ROCK**?

Digging around **FRANTICALLY**, I finally managed to pull **BRUCE** up. But he wouldn't open his eyes and he didn't respond to my attempts to revive him.

"*Bruce! Bruuuuuuuuuuuuce!*" I cried desperately. How could I lose my best friend this way? What would I do without him? He was the expert, not me!

I thought about it for a moment. Then I

knew what I had to do. I had to get Bruce back to the hut before it was too late!

I heaved him across my shoulders. Then slowly and carefully, I continued my ᴅᴇꜱᴄᴇɴᴛ.

It was hard work. Every half hour, I stopped to get my breath and check on **BRUCE**. He still seemed lifeless.

I tried going faster, huffing and puffing under Bruce's weight. Those muscles of his sure were **HEAVY**!

After about three hours, I *slid* on some rocks and fell over. For a moment, I thought I saw **BRUCE** open his eyes. But no, it must've been a **trick** of the light. He was still out.

Two hours later, I was so tired, I could hardly feel my paws. But I kept on. I had to. "**What will I do without Bruce?**" I muttered desperately.

I thought I heard someone squeak, "Don't give up! Never give up!"

I looked around in CONFUSION. But I was all alone. The only rodent nearby was Bruce, and he was still unconscious.

By the time I reached the hut, I was ready to drop. With my last ounce of *energy*, I shouted: "Hello there! Heeeeeeeelp! I've got a mouse in urgent need of medical attention!"

I huffed and puffed...

A hearty voice answered. "Medical attention? Squeak for yourself, Champ! I feel **FINE**!" With that, **BRUCE** leaped off my back and grinned at me.

I was aghast. "B-b-but . . . you're **alive**! You're all right!" I stammered.

"Of course I am! I'm always fine!" Bruce boasted. "I'm as **TOUGH** as an old sewer rat, you know that! Just much BETTER-LOOKING, of course," he added as an afterthought.

"Why did you pretend to be unconscious?" I demanded.

"First, it's **IMPORTANT** for you to get those puny muscles of yours in shape," he responded. "Secondly, it's important for you to learn to take care of yourself and others without my **HELP**. And finally, it's important for you to learn not to give up!"

I remembered that I thought I'd seen him

open his eyes and murmur, "Don't give up!"

"You had me **carry** you on my back for hours and hours!" I screeched indignantly.

Bruce smiled and nodded. "I did it for your own good," he said MADDENINGLY. "Now, where's my thank-you?"

That was the straw that **broke** this rodent's back. I chased him around and around a hut.

YOU'RE ALIVE!

Before I could catch up with that slimy excuse for a mouse, **Baraka** ran up to us with open paws. "Incredible! You're alive!"

"Of course we are," said Bruce smugly.

"There's no 'of course' about it," I protested. "I was sure we were going to become **fur coats**!"

My cell phone started *ringing*. It was **BORIS VON CACKLEFUR**.

"Geronimo, you're still alive?" he cried. "I've prepared your **COFFIN** . . . your place in the graveyard is all ready . . . if you could only see the beautiful chrysanthemums I've prepared for your **GRAVESTONE** . . ."

"Erm, thank you, Boris, that's very kind of you," I said with a shiver. "But I don't think I'll be needing —"

Suddenly, I heard a female squeak come from the other end of the phone. "Geronimo! I'm waiting for you, my little **ghoulie-whoulie**! I can't wait to make you my very own **hubby-wubby**!"

BRUCE snatched the phone from my paw. "Miss Creepella, is that you?" he roared. "Don't worry, I'll bring your beloved home to you safe and sound. Wait until you see what great shape he's in. In fact, I don't think I can call him **Cheese Puff** anymore! But if he wants the award for **T** **A** **M** (**T**ruly **A**thletic **M**ouse), I'm afraid he's got to scale another mountain: **Everest**! What do you say?"

Bruce paused. I could hear Creepella CHATTERING away on the other end. "Yes, that's just as I thought . . . Indeed, what mouse doesn't like saying that although her fiancé may look a bit of a chump, he has climbed Everest! . . . Okay, it's a deal, so now I'll take him to Everest with me, but you have to promise that I'll be the best mouse at your wedding. I'd appreciate it if you name your firstborn after me, BRUCE HYENA . . . Whaaaaat? You'd already thought of that? You are truly a kindhearted rodent, worthy of my best buddy here! Okay then, it's a deal."

He lowered his squeak. "Look, I know Stilton is a bit of an ODD rat, but if he gets

cold paws, I'll drag him to the altar by his whiskers, you have my word on that!"

With that, he snapped the phone shut. "Now don't let me down, **Cheese Puff**! I'm a rodent of my word and I don't need any *STINKY* cheese stains on my honor!"

I tried imagining my future with a wife like Creepella, a father-in-law like Boris, and a son (or daughter?) named Bruce Hyena. What a **NIGHTMARE**!

I Knew You'd Make It!

Baraka brought us certificates declaring that we'd reached the summit of **MOUNT KILIMANJARO**. He shook our paws proudly as he presented them to us.

We had a huge meal, then it was time to fly back to New Mouse City. I'd never been so happy to head home.

Benjamin greeted our plane. "Uncle Geronimo!" he cried, hugging me tightly. "I knew you'd make it to the top of **MOUNT KILIMANJARO**!"

"Benjamin!" I said happily. "This certificate is for you. I hope you'll experience an **adventure** like this yourself one day!"

CERTIFICATE OF ACHIEVEMENT

We hereby certify that the rodent

Geronimo Stilton

has climbed to the

top of Kilimanjaro.

YES, WE'RE FABUMOUSE!

When my travelogue was published in *The Rodent's Gazette*, it was **ENORMOUSELY** successful! The phones were **ringing** off the hook, and we received so many e-mails we almost **crashed** our server!

My assistant piled thousands of letters on top of my desk. "Geronimo, you have so many admirers, and they all want to meet you and **BRUCE**!" she told me.

Our fans were so energetic, the raterazzi kept trying to **break down** the doors!

All the attention made me **nervous**. Barricaded inside my office, I **peeped** out of the window. Instantly, I heard a cry: "**THERE HE IS!** It's him! It's Stilton, *Geronimo Stilton!*"

Bruce **LOOKED** out of the window, too, but he was a lot less timid than me. He blew **kisses** to his admirers. "Thank you, thank you! Yes, I know we're *fabumouse*, thank you!"

The shout that rose up from the crowd rocked the entire office.

"Bruuuuuuuuuuuuuuce!"

I went pale as the purest mozzarella. "The door is locked tight, right?" I asked my editor in chief, Kreamy O'Cheddar.

She double-checked. "Relax, Mr. Stilton, everything is under control."

I'M A VERY SHY
MOUSE . . .

I sat back down at my desk. The phone rang.

"Hello? Geronimo? It's me, **CREEPELLA!**"

"Oh, hi, Creepella," I squeaked nervously. "Sorry, I can't talk, I'm very busy."

"Nonsense, my little **creepy-crawly**. Now listen. As you know, I'm the most famouse film director on New Mouse Island, and I'm not willing to see an opportunity like this go to waste. I want to direct a movie about you and Bruce on **MOUNT KILIMANJARO.**"

"Oh, a movie?" I replied hesitantly. "Well, I'll have to think about it. I'm a very **shy** mouse, you know."

Bruce snatched the phone right out of my paw. "**OF COURSE WE'LL DO IT!**" he shouted.

I sighed. What choice did I have? Bruce would find a way to trick me into it whether I agreed or not. "Oh, all right."

I had to admit, the idea of being in a movie *was exciting*!

The movie was called ***Mighty Mount Kilimanjaro***.

Bruce wanted to go back to the summit to shoot. "Listen, **Cheese Puff**, wouldn't it be amazing to go through it all again? All that adventure, all those dangers . . ." He got a wistful look in his eyes.

Moldy mozzarella! I dashed off to the closet and locked myself in.

"No, no, no," I yelled. "You've got to be kidding! There's **NO WAY** I'm going back to **MOUNT KILIMANJARO**! I refuse to be mousenapped and dragged up that crazy mountain again!"

BRUCE knocked on the closet door. "Geronimo, I'm disappointed in you. I thought you'd changed, that you'd learned not to give up." He sighed deeply. I refused to come out until Benjamin assured me we wouldn't be returning to **MOUNT KILIMANJARO**.

CREEPELLA explained to **BRUCE** that she was going to re-create the

mountain-climbing scenes on a movie set.

Bruce was bitterly **disappointed**. "Oh, a movie set. So, no cold? No snow? No precipices? No dizzy spells? No discomfort? No risks? No death-defying dangers? No bruises, broken bones, headaches, nausea, or blisters? **What a pity.**"

I was so relieved. What could possibly happen to me in a studio?

I decided to prepare myself for the role of a lifetime. After all, how many **rodents** get to play themselves in a **MAJOR MOTION PICTURE**?

I took squeak lessons (to learn how to project my voice) and acting lessons (to learn how to **express** myself effectively). Let me tell you, actors make it look easy, but it's really **HARD**!

Yet I didn't give up. That was something I'd learned during my adventure on **KILIMANJARO: NEVER GIVE UP!** At last, the first day of filming arrived. **I was really nervous!** I put on my costume. The makeup artist combed my fur, then powdered my snout. **CREEPELLA** shouted: **"LIGHTS! CAMERA! ACTION!"** The cameramice began filming **BRUCE** and me. The editors chose the most important scenes. *And six months later, the movie was ready!*

AT THE STROKE OF MIDNIGHT

It was opening night! **BRUCE**, Benjamin, and I were invited to the premiere at New Mouse City's fanciest theater. We dressed in tuxedoes. It was the **first** time I'd ever seen Bruce wearing anything other than athletic gear. We all looked very **HANDSOME**.

The **lights** went out and the screen **CAME TO LIFE.**

From the opening sequence to the finale, the film re-created one of the most exciting **adventures** of my life. There was action, adventure, drama, suspense, and even humor. It was an AMAZING film!

When the lights came on again, applause thundered through the theater.

As we exited, rodents swarmed around us. Bruce and I signed hundreds of autographs.

Just before midnight, my good friend **Hercule Poirat** turned up. I usually try to keep him and **BRUCE** apart. They are both in **love** with my sister and they are very jealous of each other!

I started to sweat like a slice of Swiss that's been left in the sun too long. **THINGS WERE HEATING UP!**

WHO ARE YOU GOING OUT WITH TONIGHT?

The clock in the main square of New Mouse City struck midnight. *Dong! Dong! Dong! Dong! Dong! Dong! Dong! Dong! Dong! Dong! Dong! Dong!*

On the twelfth stroke, **BRUCE** looked down his snout at Hercule Poirat and said, "Hey, Cheesehead. Yeah, I'm **squeaking** to you! Your name is **Hercule**, isn't it?"

Hercule Poirat gave him a **HAUGHTY** look. "That's correct. And who might you be?"

"**BRUCE!**"

"Bruce who?"

"Just **BRUCE** to you!"

I tried to calm them both down. "Um, yes, well, I'm really glad my two best **FRIENDS** have at last had the chance to meet."

But they weren't listening. They were glaring at each other.

BRUCE put on his toughest **he-mouse** look.

Hercule responded with his **brainiest**, most superior smirk.

At that moment, Thea strolled in.

"*Thea,*" **BRUCE** said, sighing. His whiskers were trembling with emotion and devotion.

"*Thea*,"
whispered
Hercule.

A silly look came over his snout.

My sister gave them each a 𝕤𝕒𝕤𝕤𝕪 smile.

I rolled my eyes and sighed in relief. I know my sister like the back of my paw.

"Thea, who are you going out with tonight?" cried Bruce and Hercule together.

Thea twirled her whiskers flirtatiously. "Well, I already have a date with 𝕙𝕚𝕞!"

A conceited-looking rodent stood behind my sister. He was handsome, all right, but he had an **arrogant** air about him that really rubbed my fur the wrong way.

He *kissed* Thea on the back of the paw and said smoothly, "Well, my darling, let us make haste. Our automobile awaits!"

With that, the two of them set off in the

direction of a **LUXURY YELLOW SPORTSCAR** with synthetic cat-fur seats.

Thea waved bye-bye, and the **raterazzi** went wild. "That's Igor Snob, the biggest name in **MOUSEYWOOD** at the moment. He's just been awarded a **Ratscar**!" whispered the gossip columnist next to us.

"Well, I'll be a tomcat's uncle!" I **squeaked** worriedly. I hoped Thea wasn't taking the whole thing SERIOUSLY. I certainly didn't fancy having Igor for a brother-in-law!

BRUCE and **Hercule** looked at each other. I thought they were going to start ARGUING again. Instead, they threw their paws around each other and began SOBBING. "We've lost her forever!" cried Bruce.

I had an idea. "I know, let's go to my favorite French restaurant in town, **Le squeakery**. We can drown our sorrows in their special cheddar fondue!"

Hercule brightened up at once. "Fondue? Elementary, my dear Stilton! What a fabumouse idea!"

"Fondue?" Bruce roared. "That'll be hard on the waistline but easy on the heart, cheese puff!"

THERE'S NOTHING LIKE CHEESE . . .

At **Le squeakery**, we got a cozy little table in the back. "**Now, are you two going to make peace?**" I demanded.

Bruce shook his snout. "Not peace, no . . ." he began.

"But we can manage a truce!" Hercule finished.

They shook paws, then stuck their snouts in the **special** cheeses menu, squeaking away like there was no tomorrow. I grinned

behind my whiskers. There's nothing like
C H E E S E to make peace among mice.

We were greedily guzzling down a
big pot of fondue when I heard a sweet
voice call: "Geronimo! I saw your film!
CONGRATULATIONS!"

It was Makeda!

I nearly choked on the piece of bread I
had just dunked into the boiling fondue.
"AAAAAAAAAAAGGGGGGGHHHHHHH!"

Tears welled up in my eyes. (Not tears of
emotion, tears of pain — that fondue was
really hot!) But I wasn't about to lose
another opportunity with Makeda.

Gathering up my courage, I scampered
over to her table. "**Makeda**, you
have no idea how much I've been
thinking about you." I bowed and
kissed her soft paw.

AH, LOVE!

Makeda smiled **sweetly**. "I've been thinking about you too, Geronimo."

"*R-r-really?*" I stammered. "H-h-have you really?"

She nodded. "Yes. I have a proposal for you, Geronimo."

"Yeeeeeees! Anything for you! Go ahead, what do you propose?"

Makeda gave me an earnest look. "*Would you like to climb Everest with me?*"

Me? Climb Everest?? Again???

Me? Climb **EVEREST**? Again? As you know, I've been to Everest before, but I didn't make it to the top. In fact, I was kidnapped by a YETI. A real, live YETI!!

I looked Makeda in the eyes. A wave of uncontrollable emotion swept over me. I'd do anything for her.

Ah, *love*! That's how it always goes. A mouse will do anything for the object of his affection.

Do you want to know what happened in the end?

Well, I really did climb **EVEREST**! And this time, I made it all the way to the top. That's right. Holey cheese, I reached the top of the world's highest mountain!

But, dear readers, that's a story for another day — and another *adventure*!

Want to read my next adventure?
I can't wait to tell you all about it!

THE PECULIAR
PUMPKIN THIEF

Halloween is a few days away when all of the pumpkins in New Mouse City disappear! There's a thief on the loose, and the thief wants to stop Halloween. Can my detective friend Hercule Poirat and I solve the mystery in time to save Halloween?

And don't miss any of my other fabumouse adventures!

#1 LOST TREASURE OF THE EMERALD EYE

#2 THE CURSE OF THE CHEESE PYRAMID

#3 CAT AND MOUSE IN A HAUNTED HOUSE

#4 I'M TOO FOND OF MY FUR!

#5 FOUR MICE DEEP IN THE JUNGLE

#6 PAWS OFF, CHEDDARFACE!

#7 RED PIZZAS FOR A BLUE COUNT

#8 ATTACK OF THE BANDIT CATS

#9 A FABUMOUSE VACATION FOR GERONIMO

#10 ALL BECAUSE OF A CUP OF COFFEE

11 IT'S HALLOWEEN, YOU 'FRAIDY MOUSE!

#12 MERRY CHRISTMAS, GERONIMO!

#13 THE PHANTOM OF THE SUBWAY

#14 THE TEMPLE OF THE RUBY OF FIRE

#15 THE MONA MOUSA CODE

#16 A CHEESE-COLORED CAMPER

#17 WATCH YOUR WHISKERS, STILTON!

#18 SHIPWRECK ON THE PIRATE ISLANDS

#19 MY NAME IS STILTON, GERONIMO STILTON

#20 SURF'S UP, GERONIMO!

#21 THE WILD, WILD WEST

#22 THE SECRET OF CACKLEFUR CASTLE

A CHRISTMAS TALE

#23 VALENTINE'S DAY DISASTER

#24 FIELD TRIP TO NIAGARA FALLS

#25 THE SEARCH FOR SUNKEN TREASURE

#26 THE MUMMY WITH NO NAME

#27 THE CHRISTMAS TOY FACTORY

#28 WEDDING CRASHER

#29 DOWN AND OUT DOWN UNDER

#30 THE MOUSE
ISLAND MARATHON

#31 THE MYSTERIOUS
CHEESE THIEF

CHRISTMAS
CATASTROPHE

#32 VALLEY OF THE
GIANT SKELETONS

#33 GERONIMO
AND THE GOLD
MEDAL MYSTERY

#34 GERONIMO
STILTON, SECRET
AGENT

#35 A VERY
MERRY CHRISTMAS

#36 GERONIMO'S
VALENTINE

#37 THE RACE
ACROSS AMERICA

#38 A FABUMOUSE
SCHOOL
ADVENTURE

#39 SINGING
SENSATION

#40 THE KARATE
MOUSE

#41 MIGHTY MOUNT
KILIMANJARO

*And don't
forget to
look for*

#42 THE PECULIAR
PUMPKIN THIEF

If you like my brother's books, check out the next adventure of the Thea Sisters!

THEA STILTON AND THE SECRET CITY

In this amazing adventure, the Thea Sisters head to Peru, where a good friend of Paulina's is in danger. There, the five mice climb the Andes mountains in search of a mysterious treasure that's hidden in the Secret City of the Incas.

Be sure to check out these other exciting Thea Sisters adventures:

ABOUT THE AUTHOR

Born in New Mouse City, Mouse Island, **GERONIMO**
STILTON is Rattus Emeritus of Mousomorphic Literature and of Neo-Ratonic Comparative Philosophy. For the past twenty years, he has been running *The Rodent's Gazette*, New Mouse City's most widely read daily newspaper.

Stilton was awarded the Ratitzer Prize for his scoops on *The Curse of the Cheese Pyramid* and *The Search for Sunken Treasure*. He has also received the Andersen 2000 Prize for Personality of the Year. One of his bestsellers won the 2002 eBook Award for world's best ratlings' electronic book. His works have been published all over the globe.

In his spare time, Mr. Stilton collects antique cheese rinds and plays golf. But what he most enjoys is telling stories to his nephew Benjamin.

Illustration by **Evelyn Bruno**, a third grader at Public School 58, Staten Island, New York

THE RODENT'S GAZETTE

1. Main entrance
2. Printing presses (where the books and newspaper are printed)
3. Accounts department
4. Editorial room (where the editors, illustrators, and designers work)
5. Geronimo Stilton's office
6. Storage space for Geronimo's books

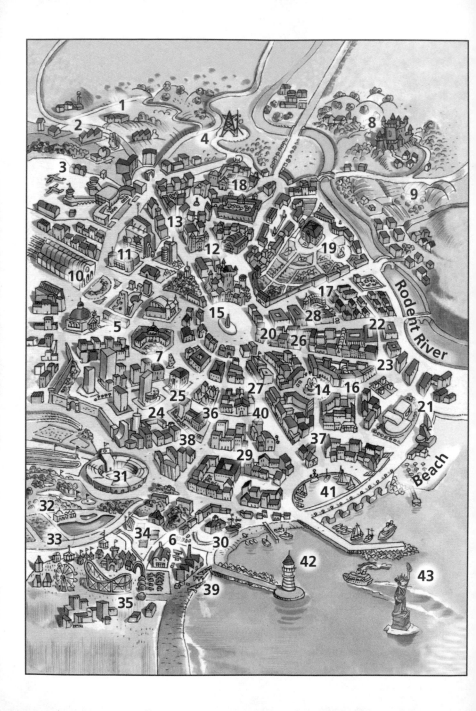

Map of New Mouse City

1. Industrial Zone
2. Cheese Factories
3. Angorat International Airport
4. WRAT Radio and Television Station
5. Cheese Market
6. Fish Market
7. Town Hall
8. Snotnose Castle
9. The Seven Hills of Mouse Island
10. Mouse Central Station
11. Trade Center
12. Movie Theater
13. Gym
14. Catnegie Hall
15. Singing Stone Plaza
16. The Gouda Theater
17. Grand Hotel
18. Mouse General Hospital
19. Botanical Gardens
20. Cheap Junk for Less (Trap's store)
21. Parking Lot
22. Mouseum of Modern Art
23. University and Library
24. *The Daily Rat*
25. *The Rodent's Gazette*
26. Trap's House
27. Fashion District
28. The Mouse House Restaurant
29. Environmental Protection Center
30. Harbor Office
31. Mousidon Square Garden
32. Golf Course
33. Swimming Pool
34. Blushing Meadow Tennis Courts
35. Curlyfur Island Amusement Park
36. Geronimo's House
37. New Mouse City Historic District
38. Public Library
39. Shipyard
40. Thea's House
41. New Mouse Harbor
42. Luna Lighthouse
43. The Statue of Liberty

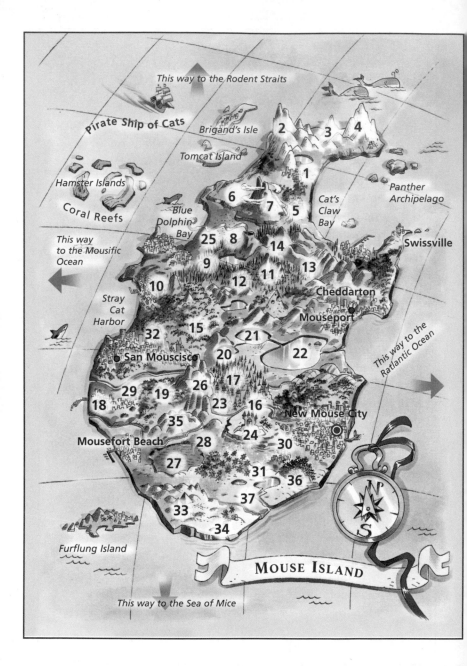

Map of Mouse Island

Dear mouse friends,
Thanks for reading, and farewell
till the next book.
It'll be another whisker-licking-good
adventure, and that's a promise!

Geronimo Stilton